Tove

Jansson

Moomintrolls and Friends

PENGUIN BOOKS

PENGUIN BOOKS

Published by the Penguin Group
Penguin Books Ltd, 27 Wrights Lane, London W8 5TZ, England
Penguin Books USA Inc., 375 Hudson Street, New York, New York 10014, USA
Penguin Books Australia Ltd, Ringwood, Victoria, Australia
Penguin Books Canada Ltd, 10 Alcorn Avenue, Toronto, Ontario, Canada M4V 3B2
Penguin Books (NZ) Ltd, 182–190 Wairau Road, Auckland 10, New Zealand
Penguin Books Ltd, Registered Offices: Harmondsworth, Middlesex, England

First published in *Det Osynliga* in Finland 1962
This translation published in *Tales from Moominvalley* by Ernest Benn in Great Britain and by Henry Z. Walck in the USA 1963
Published in Puffin Books 1973

This collection published in Penguin Books 1996
1 3 5 7 9 10 8 6 4 2

Set in 11.5/13pt Bembo Monotype
Typeset by Datix International Ltd, Bungay, Suffolk
Printed in England by Clays Ltd, St Ives plc

Contents

The Secret of the Hattifatteners

ONCE upon a time, rather long ago, it so happened that Moominpappa went away from home without the least explanation and without even himself understanding why he had to go.

Moominmamma said afterwards that he had seemed odd for quite a time, but probably he hadn't been odder than usual. That was just one of those things one thinks up afterwards when one's bewildered and sad and wants the comfort of an explanation.

No one was quite certain of the moment Moominpappa had left.

Snufkin said that he had intended to row out with the hemulen to catch some alburn, but according to the hemulen Moominpappa had only sat on the verandah as usual and suddenly remarked that the weather was hot and boring and that the landing-stage needed a bit of repair. In any case Moominpappa hadn't repaired it, because it was as lop-sided as before. Also the boat was still there.

So Moominpappa had set out on foot, and as he

could have chosen several directions there was no point in looking for him.

'He'll be back in due time,' Moominmamma said. 'That's what he used to tell me from the beginning, and he always came back, so I suppose he'll return this time too.'

No one felt worried, and that was a good thing. They had decided never to feel worried about each other; in this way everybody was helped to a good conscience and as much freedom as possible.

So Moominmamma started some new knitting without making any fuss, and somewhere to the west Moominpappa was wandering along with a dim idea firmly in his head.

It had to do with a cape he once had seen on one of the family picnics. The cape had pointed straight out to sea, the sky had been yellow and a bit of wind had sprung up towards night. He had never been able to go out there to see what was on the other side. The family wanted to turn home for tea. They always wanted to go home at the wrong time. But Moominpappa had stood on the beach for a while, looking out over the water. And at that very

moment a row of small white boats with sprit sails

had come into sight under land, putting straight out to sea.

'That's hattifatteners,' the hemulen had said, and in those words everything was expressed. A little slightingly, a little cautiously and quite clearly with repudiation. Those were the outsiders, half-dangerous, different.

And then an overpowering longing and melancholy had gripped Moominpappa, and the only thing he knew for certain was that he didn't want any tea on the verandah. Not that evening, nor any other evening.

This had been quite a time ago, but the picture never left him. And so one afternoon he went away.

The day was hot, and he walked at random.

He didn't dare to think about it, nor to feel anything, he simply went on walking towards the sunset, screwing up his eyes under the hatbrim and whistling to himself, but no special tune. There were uphills and downhills, the trees came wandering towards and past him, and their shadows were beginning to lengthen.

At the moment when the sun dipped down into the sea Moominpappa came out on to the long gravel shore where no ways ever stopped and no one ever thought of going for a picnic.

He hadn't seen it before; it was a grey and dreary beach that told him nothing except that land ended and sea started here. Moominpappa stepped down to the water and looked outward.

And naturally – what else could indeed have happened? – at that very moment a little white boat came slowly gliding before the wind along the shore.

'Here they are,' Moominpappa said calmly and started to wave.

There were only three hattifatteners aboard the boat. They were quite as white as the boat and the sail. One was sitting at the helm and two with their backs to the mast. All three were staring out to sea and looking as if they had been quarrelling. But Moominpappa had heard that hattifatteners never quarrel, they are very silent and interested only in travelling onwards, as far as possible. All the way to the horizon, or to the world's end, which is probably the same thing. Or so people said. It was also said that a hattifattener cared for nothing but himself, and further that they all became electric in a thunderstorm.

 Also that they were dangerous company to all who

lived in drawing-rooms and verandahs and were used to doing certain things at certain times.

All this had greatly interested Moominpappa for as long as he could remember, but as it isn't considered quite nice to talk about hattifatteners, except indirectly, he still didn't know whether all those things were true.

Now he felt a shiver from head to tail and in great excitement saw the boat draw nearer. The hattifatteners did not signal to him in reply – one couldn't even imagine them making such large and everyday gestures – but it was quite clear that they were coming for him. With a faint rustling their boat ploughed into the gravel and lay still.

The hattifatteners turned their round, pale eyes to Moominpappa. He tipped his hat and started to explain. While he spoke the hattifatteners' paws started to wave about in time to his words, and this made Moominpappa perplexed. He suddenly found himself hopelessly tangled up in a long sentence about horizons, verandahs, freedom and drinking tea when one doesn't want any tea. At last he stopped in embarrassment, and the hattifatteners' paws stopped also.

Why don't they say anything? Moominpappa thought nervously. Can't they hear me, or do they think I'm silly?

He offered his paw and made a friendly, interrogatory noise, but the hattifatteners didn't move. Only their eyes slowly changed colour and became yellow as the evening sky.

Moominpappa drew his paw back and made a clumsy bow.

The hattifatteners at once rose and bowed in reply, very solemnly, all three at the same time.

'A pleasure,' Moominpappa said.

He made no other effort to explain things, but clambered aboard and thrust off. The sky was burning yellow, exactly as it had been that other time. The boat started on a slow outward tack.

Never in his life had Moominpappa felt so at ease and pleased with everything. He found it splendid for a change not to have to say anything or explain anything, to himself or to others. He could simply sit looking at the horizon listening to the cluck of the water.

When the coast had disappeared a full moon rose, round and yellow over the sea. Never before had

Moominpappa seen such a large and lonely moon. And never before had he grasped that the sea could be as absolute and enormous as he saw it now.

All at once he had a feeling, that the only real and convincing things in existence were the moon and the sea and the boat, with the three silent hattifatteners.

And the horizon, of course – the horizon in the distance where splendid adventures and nameless secrets were waiting for him, now that he was free at last.

He decided to become silent and mysterious, like a hattifattener. People respected one if one didn't talk. They believed that one knew a great many things and led a very exciting life.

Moominpappa looked at the hattifatteners at the helm. He felt like saying something chummy, something to show he understood. But then he let it alone. Anyway, he didn't find any words that – well, that would have sounded right.

What was it the Mymble had said about hattifatteners? Last spring, at dinner one day. That they led a wicked life. And Moominmamma had said: That's just talk: but My became enormously interested and wanted to know what it meant. As far as Moomin-pappa could remember no one had been really able to describe what people did when they led a wicked life. Probably they behaved wildly and freely in a general way.

Moominmamma had said that she didn't even believe that a wicked life was any fun, but Moomin-pappa hadn't been quite sure. It's got something to do with electricity, the Mymble had said, cocksurely. And they're able to read people's thoughts, and that's not allowed. Then the talk had turned to other things.

Moominpappa gave the hattifatteners a quick look. They were waving their paws again. Oh, how horrible, he thought. Can it be that they're sitting there reading my thoughts with their paws? And now they're hurt, of course . . . He tried desperately to smooth out all his thoughts, clear them out of the way, forget all he had ever heard about hattifatteners, but it wasn't easy. At the moment nothing else interested him. If he could only talk to them. It was such a good way to keep one from thinking.

And it was no use to leave the great dangerous thoughts aside and concentrate on the small and friendly sort. Because then the hattifatteners might think that they were mistaken and that he was only an ordinary verandah Moominpappa . . .

Moominpappa strained his eyes looking out over the sea towards a small black cliff that showed in the moonlight.

He tried to think quite simple thoughts: there's an island in the sea, the moon's directly above it, the moon's swimming in the water – coal-black, yellow, dark blue. At last he calmed down again, and the hattifatteners stopped their waving.

The island was very steep, although small.

Knobbly and dark it rose from the water, not very unlike the head of one of the larger sea-serpents.

'Do we land?' Moominpappa asked.

The hattifatteners didn't reply. They stepped ashore with the painter and made fast in a crevice. Without giving him a glance they started to climb up the shore. He could see them sniffing against the wind, and then bowing and waving in some deep conspiracy that left him outside.

'Never mind me,' Moominpappa exclaimed in a hurt voice and clambered ashore. 'But if I ask you if we're going to land, even if I see that we are, you might still give me a civil answer. Just a word or two, so I feel I've company.'

But he said this only under his breath, and strictly to himself.

The cliff was steep and slippery. It was an unfriendly island that told everyone quite clearly to keep out. It had no flowers, no moss, nothing – it just thrust itself out of the water with an angry look.

All at once Moominpappa made a very strange and disagreeable discovery. The island was full of red spiders. They were quite small but innumerable, swarming over the black cliff like a live red carpet.

Not one of them was sitting still, everyone was rushing about for all his worth. The whole island seemed to be crawling in the moonlight.

It made Moominpappa feel quite weak.

He lifted his legs, he quickly rescued his tail and shook it thoroughly, he stared about him for a single spot empty of red spiders, but there was none.

'I don't want to tread on you,' Moominpappa mumbled. 'Dear me, why didn't I remain in the boat . . . They're too many, it's unnatural to be so many of the same kind . . . all of them exactly alike.'

He looked helplessly for the hattifatteners and

caught sight of their silhouettes against the moon, high up on the cliff. One of them had found something. Moominpappa couldn't see what it was.

No difference to him, anyway. He went back to the boat, shaking his paws like a cat. Some of the spiders had crawled on to him, and he thought it very unpleasant.

They soon found the painter also and started to crawl along it in a thin red procession, and from there further along the gunwale.

Moominpappa seated himself as far astern as possible.

This is something one dreams, he thought. And then one awakens with a jerk to tell Moominmamma: 'You can't imagine how horrible, dearest, such a lot of spiders, you never . . .'

And she awakens too and replies: 'Oh, poor Pappa – that was a dream, there aren't any spiders here . . .'

The hattifatteners were slowly returning.

Immediately every spider jumped high with fright, turned and ran back ashore along the painter.

The hattifatteners came aboard and pushed off. The boat glided out from the black shadow of the island, into the moonlight.

'Glory be that you're back!' Moominpappa cried with great relief. 'As a matter of fact I've never liked spiders that are too small to talk with. Did you find anything interesting?'

The hattifatteners gave him a long moon-yellow look and remained silent.

'I said did you find anything,' Moominpappa repeated, a little red in the snout. 'If it's a secret of course you can keep it to yourselves. But at least tell me there *was* something.'

The hattifatteners were quite still and silent, only looking at him. At this Moominpappa felt his head grow hot and cried:

'Do you like spiders? Do you like them or not? I want to know at once!'

In the long ensuing silence one of the hattifatteners took a step forward and spread its paws. Perhaps it had replied something – or else it was just a whisper from the wind.

'I'm sorry,' Moominpappa said uncertainly, 'I see.' He felt that the hattifattener had explained to him that they had no special attitude to spiders. Or else it had deplored something that could not be helped.

 Perhaps the sad fact that a hattifattener and a Moominpappa will never be able to tell each other anything. Perhaps it was disappointed in Moominpappa and thought him rather childish. He sighed and gave them a downcast look. Now he could see what they had found. It was a small scroll of birch-bark, of the sort the sea likes to curl up and throw ashore. Nothing else. You can unroll them like documents: inside they're white and silk-smooth, and as soon as they're released they curl shut again. Exactly like a small fist clasped about a secret. Moominmamma used to keep one around the handle of her tea-kettle.

Probably this scroll contained some important message or other. But Moominpappa wasn't really curious any longer. He was a little cold, and curled up on the floor of the boat for a nap. The hattifatteners never felt any cold, only electricity.

And they never slept.

Moominpappa awoke by dawn. He felt stiff in the back and still rather cold. From under his hatbrim he could see part of the gunwale and a grey triangle of sea falling and rising and falling again. He was feeling a little sick, and not at all like an adventurous Moomin.

One of the hattifatteners was sitting on the nearest

thwart, and he observed it surreptitiously. Now its eyes were grey. The paws were very finely cut. They were flexing slowly, like the wings of a sitting moth. Perhaps the hattifattener was talking to its fellows, or just thinking. Its head was round and quite neckless. Most of all he resembles a long white sock, Moominpappa thought. A little frayed at the lower, open end, and as if made of white foam rubber.

Now he was feeling a little sicker still. He remembered his behaviour of last night. And those spiders. It was the first time he had seen a spider frightened.

'Dear, dear,' Moominpappa mumbled. He was about to sit up, but then he caught sight of the birch-bark scroll and stiffened. He pricked his ears under the hat. The scroll lay in the bailer on the floor, slowly rolling with the movement of the boat.

Moominpappa forgot all about seasickness. His paw cautiously crept out. He gave the hattifatteners a quick look and saw that their eyes as usual were fixed on the horizon. Now he had the scroll, he closed his paw around it, he pulled it towards him. At that moment he felt a slight electric shock, no stronger than from a flashlight battery when you feel it with your tongue. But he hadn't been prepared for it.

He lay still for a long time, calming himself. Then started slowly to unroll the secret document. It turned out to be ordinary white birch-bark. No treasure map. No code letter. Nothing.

Perhaps it was just a kind of visiting card, politely left on every lone island by every hattifattener, to be found by other hattifatteners? Perhaps that little electric shock gave them the same friendly and sociable feeling one gets from a nice letter? Or perhaps they had an invisible writing unknown to ordinary trolls? Moominpappa disappointedly let the birch-bark curl itself back into a scroll again, and looked up.

The hattifatteners were regarding him calmly. Moominpappa reddened.

'We're all in the same boat, anyway,' he said. And without expecting any reply he spread his paws like he had seen the hattifatteners do, in a helpless and regretful gesture, and sighed.

To this the wind replied with a faint howl in the tight stays. The sea was rolling grey waves all the way to the world's end, and Moominpappa thought with some sadness: If this is a wicked life I'd rather eat my hat.

★

There are many kinds of island, but all those that are small enough and far enough are without exception rather sad and lonesome. The winds chase all around them, the yellow moon increases and wanes again, the sea becomes coal-black every night, but the islands are always unchanged and only hattifatteners visit them now and then. They are not even real islands. They are skerries, rocks, reefs, forgotten streaks of land that perhaps even sink under water before daybreak and rise over the surface again during the night to take a look around. One can't know.

The hattifatteners visited them all. Sometimes a birch-bark scroll was there waiting for them. Sometimes there was nothing; the islet was just a smooth seal's back surrounded by breakers, or a ragged rock with high banks of red sea-weed. But on the summit of every island the hattifatteners left behind them a small white scroll.

They have an idea, Moominpappa thought. Something that's more important to them than all other matters. And I'm going to follow them about until I know what it is.

They met no more red spiders, but Moominpappa

remained aboard every time they landed. Because

those islands made him think of other islands far behind him, the picnic islands, the green and leafy bathing inlets, the tent, and the butter container cooling in the shadow by the boat, the juice glasses in the sand, and the bathing-trunks adry on a sun-hot boulder . . . Not that he missed that kind of secure verandah life for a minute. Those were just thoughts that came flapping past and made him a bit sad. Thoughts about small and insignificant things.

As a matter of fact Moominpappa had started to think in a wholly new manner. Less and less often he mused about things he had encountered in his kindly and chequered life, and quite as seldom did he dream about what his future would bring him.

His thoughts glided along like the boat, without memories or dreams, they were like grey wandering waves that didn't even want to reach the horizon.

Moominpappa stopped trying to talk to the hatti-fatteners. He sat staring seawards, just as they did, his eyes had turned pale like theirs, taking the colour of the sky. And when new islands swam into view he didn't even move, only tapped his tail once or twice against the floor.

Once, as they glided along on the back of a slow,

tired swell, Moominpappa fleetingly thought: I wonder if I'm beginning to resemble a hattifattener.

It had been a very hot day, and towards evening a mist rolled in from the sea. It was a heavy, curiously reddish mist. Moominpappa thought it looked menacing and a little alive.

The sea-serpents were snorting and wallowing far out, he could catch a glimpse of them at times. A round, dark head, startled eyes staring at the hattifatteners, then a splash from a tail fin and a quick flight back into the mist.

They're afraid like the spiders were, Moominpappa thought. Everyone's afraid of hattifatteners . . .

A far-away thunderclap went rolling through the silence, and everything was quiet and immobile once more.

Moominpappa always had thought thunderstorms very exciting. Now he didn't have any opinion about them. He was quite free, but he just didn't seem to have any likings any more.

At that moment a strange boat steered out of the mist with a large company aboard. Moominpappa jumped to his feet. In a moment he had become the old Moominpappa again, waving his hat about and shouting. The strange boat was coming straight towards them. It was white, the sail was white. And the people aboard it were white . . .

'Oh, I see,' Moominpappa said. He sat down again. The two boats continued their courses without exchanging any greeting.

And then one boat after the other glided out of the dark mist, all going the same way and all manned by hattifatteners. Sometimes by seven, sometimes by five, or eleven, at times even by one solitary hattifattener, but always by an odd number.

The mist cleared away and rolled into the slightly reddish evening dusk. The sea seemed to be packed with boats. All were on their way towards a new island, a low skerry with no trees and no high cliffs.

The thunder went rolling over again. It was hiding somewhere in the enormous black cloud that was now climbing higher and higher over the horizon.

One boat after the other put in and lowered sail. The lonely beach was already thronged by hattifatteners that had arrived earlier and were standing bowing to each other.

As far as one could see, white solemn beings were

walking about and exchanging bows to right and left. They emitted a faint rustling sound and were constantly waving their paws. The beach grass whispered around them.

Moominpappa was standing aside by himself. He tried desperately to find his own hattifatteners among the crowd. He felt it to be important. They were the only ones he knew . . . slightly. Very slightly. But still.

They had disappeared in the throng, he could see no differences in the many hundreds of hattifatteners, and all at once Moominpappa was caught by the same terror as on the spider island. He pulled his hat down to his eyebrows and tried to look tough and at ease at the same time.

His hat was the only fixed and absolute thing on this strange island where all was white and whispering and vague.

Moominpappa didn't quite trust himself any longer, but he believed in his hat; it was black and resolute, and inside it Moominmamma had painted the words 'M.P. from your M.M.' to distinguish it from all other high hats in the world.

Now the last boat had landed and been pulled

ashore, and the hattifatteners stopped rustling. They turned their reddish eyes towards Moominpappa, all together, and the next instant they began to move in his direction.

They want to fight, Moominpappa thought, and was suddenly wide awake and rather elated. In that moment he felt like fighting anyone just to fight and shout and feel sure that everyone else was wrong and deserving a good hiding.

Only hattifatteners never fight, nor do they object to anything or dislike anyone or hold any opinion at all.

They came to exchange bows with Moominpappa, all the hundreds of them, and Moominpappa tipped his hat and bowed in reply until he felt a headache coming on. Hundreds of paws waved at him until he also began waving his from sheer exhaustion.

When the last hattifattener had passed him Moominpappa had forgotten all about wanting a fight. His mind was polite and smooth, and he followed the others, hat in hand, through the whispering grass.

The thunderstorm had climbed high in the meantime and was hovering in the sky like a wall about to fall down. High up a wind was blowing, driving small rugged tufts of cloud before it in scared flight.

Close to the sea sudden and fitful lightning was flashing, switching off and flaring up again.

The hattifatteners had assembled in the centre of the island. They had turned southwards, where the thunderstorm waited, exactly like seabirds before a gale. One after the other they began to light up like little lamp bulbs, flaring in time with the lightning. The grass around them was crackling with electricity.

Moominpappa had laid himself on his back and was staring up at the pale green leaves around him. Light, delicate leaves against a dark sky. In his easy-chair at home he had a cushion embroidered with fern leaves by Moominmamma. Pale green leaves against black felt. It was very beautiful.

The thunderstorm was nearing rapidly. Moominpappa felt faint shocks in his paws and sat up. There was rain in the air.

All of a sudden the hattifatteners began fluttering their paws like moth wings. They were all swaying, bowing and dancing, and a thin, gnat-like song arose from the lonely island. It was the howl of the hattifatteners, a lonely and yearning sound like wind in a bottleneck. Moominpappa felt an irresistible desire to do as the hattifatteners did. To sway back and forth, to sway and howl and rustle.

He felt a prickle in his ears, and his paws began to wave. He rose to his feet and started to walk towards the hattifatteners. Their secret's got to do with thunderstorms, he thought. It's thunderstorms they are always looking for and longing for . . .

Darkness fell over the island, and the lightning flashes were running straight down from the sky, like streams of dangerously white and hissing liquid. Far out the wind started to roar, and then the thunder broke loose, the fiercest thunder Moominpappa had ever experienced.

Heavy wagons of stone were rolling and rumbling back and forth, to and fro, and the wind caught hold of Moominpappa and threw him back in the grass.

He sat holding his hat and feeling the wind blow through him, and all of a sudden he thought: No. What's come over me? I'm no hattifattener, I'm Moominpappa . . . What am I doing here?

He looked at the hattifatteners, and with electric simplicity he understood it all. He grasped that only a great thunderstorm could put some life in hattifatteners. They were heavily charged but hopelessly locked up. They didn't feel, they didn't think – they could only seek. Only in the presence of electricity they were able to live at last, strongly and with great and intense feelings.

That was what they longed for. Perhaps they were even able to attract a thunderstorm when they assembled in large crowds . . .

Yes, that must be the solution, Moominpappa thought. Poor hattifatteners. And I was sitting on my verandah believing they were so remarkable and free, just because they never spoke a word and were always on the move. They hadn't a single word to say and nowhere to go . . .

The skies opened and the rain crashed down, gleaming white in the flashes of lightning.

Moominpappa jumped to his feet. His eyes were as blue as ever, and he shouted:

'I'm going home! I'm leaving at once!'

He stuck his snout in the air and pulled his hat securely over his ears. Then he ran down to the beach, jumped aboard one of the white boats, hoisted sail and put straight out to the stormy sea.

He was himself once again, he had his own thoughts about things, and he longed to be home.

Just think, never to be glad nor disappointed, Moominpappa mused while the boat was carried along in the gale. Never to like anyone and get cross at him and forgive him. Never to sleep or feel cold, never to make a mistake and have a belly-ache and be cured from it, never to have a birthday party, drink beer and have a bad conscience . . .

How terrible.

He felt happy and drenched and not in the least afraid of the thunderstorm. At home they would never have electric light, he decided, they'd keep the old kerosene lamps.

Moominpappa longed for his family and his verandah. All of a sudden he thought that at home he could be just as free and adventurous as a real pappa should be.

The Invisible Child

ONE dark and rainy evening the Moomin family sat around the verandah table picking over the day's mushroom harvest. The big table was covered with newspapers, and in the centre of it stood the lighted kerosene lamp. But the corners of the verandah were dark.

'My has been picking pepper spunk again,' Moominpappa said. 'Last year she collected flybane.'

'Let's hope she takes to chanterelles next autumn,' said Moominmamma. 'Or at least to something not directly poisonous.'

'Hope for the best and prepare for the worst,' little My observed with a chuckle.

They continued their work in peaceful silence.

Suddenly there were a few light taps on the glass pane in the door, and without waiting for an answer Too-ticky came in and shook the rain off her oilskin jacket. Then she held the door open and called out in the dark: 'Well, come along!'

'Whom are you bringing?' Moomintroll asked.

'It's Ninny,' Too-ticky said. 'Yes, her name's Ninny.'

She still held the door open, waiting. No one came.

'Oh, well,' Too-ticky said and shrugged her shoulders. 'If she's too shy she'd better stay there for a while.'

'She'll be drenched through,' said Moominmamma.

'Perhaps that won't matter much when one's invisible,' Too-ticky said and sat down by the table. The family stopped working and waited for an explanation.

'You all know, don't you, that if people are frightened very often, they sometimes become invisible,' Too-ticky said and swallowed a small egg mushroom that looked like a little snowball. 'Well. This Ninny was frightened the wrong way by a lady who had taken care of her without really liking her. I've met this lady, and she was horrid. Not the angry sort, you know, which would have been understandable. No, she was the icily ironical kind.'

'What's ironical?' Moomintroll asked.

'Well, imagine that you slip on a rotten mushroom and sit down on the basket of newly picked ones,' Too-ticky said. 'The natural thing for your mother would be to be angry. But no, she isn't. Instead she says, very coldly: "I understand that's your idea of a graceful dance, but I'd thank you not to do it in people's food." Something like that.'

'How unpleasant,' Moomintroll said.

'Yes, isn't it,' replied Too-ticky. 'This was the way this lady used to talk. She was ironic all day long every day, and finally the kid started to turn pale and fade around the edges, and less and less was seen of her. Last Friday one couldn't catch sight of her at all. The lady gave her away to me and said she really couldn't take care of relatives she couldn't even see.'

'And what did you do to the lady?' My asked with bulging eyes. 'Did you bash her head?'

'That's of no use with the ironic sort,' Too-ticky said. 'I took Ninny home with me, of course. And now I've brought her here for you to make her visible again.'

There was a slight pause. Only the rain was heard, rustling along over the verandah roof. Everybody stared at Too-ticky and thought for a while.

'Does she talk?' Moominpappa asked.

'No. But the lady has hung a small silver bell around her neck so that one can hear where she is.'

Too-ticky arose and opened the door again. 'Ninny!' she called out in the dark.

The cool smell of autumn crept in from the garden, and a square of light threw itself on the wet grass. After a while there was a slight tinkle outside, rather hesitantly. The sound came up the steps and stopped. A bit above the floor a small silver bell was seen hanging in the air on a black ribbon. Ninny seemed to have a very thin neck.

'All right,' Too-ticky said. 'Now, here's your new family. They're a bit silly at times, but rather decent, largely speaking.'

'Give the kid a chair,' Moominpappa said. 'Does she know how to pick mushrooms?'

'I really know nothing at all about Ninny,' Too-ticky said. 'I've only brought her here and told you what I know. Now I have a few other things to attend to. Please look in some day, won't you, and let me know how you get along. Cheerio.'

When Too-ticky had gone the family sat quite silent, looking at the empty chair and the silver bell. After a while one of the chanterelles slowly rose from the heap on the table. Invisible paws picked it clean from needles and earth. Then it was cut to pieces, and the pieces drifted away and laid themselves in the basin. Another mushroom sailed up from the table.

'Thrilling!' My said with awe. 'Try to give her something to eat. I'd like to know if you can see the food when she swallows it.'

'How on earth does one make her visible again?' Moominpappa said worriedly. 'Should we take her to a doctor?'

'I don't think so,' said Moominmamma. 'I believe she wants to be invisible for a while. Too-ticky said she's shy. Better leave the kid alone until something turns up.'

And so it was decided.

The eastern attic room happened to be unoccupied, so Moominmamma made Ninny a bed there. The silver bell tinkled along after her upstairs and reminded Moominmamma of the cat that once had lived with them. At the bedside she laid out the apple, the glass of juice and the three striped pieces of candy everybody in the house was given at bedtime.

Then she lighted a candle and said:

'Now have a good sleep, Ninny. Sleep as late as you can. There'll be tea for you in the morning any time you want. And if you happen to get a funny feeling or if you want anything, just come downstairs and tinkle.'

Moominmamma saw the quilt raise itself to form a very small mound. A dent appeared in the pillow. She went downstairs again to her own room and started looking through her granny's old notes about Infallible Household Remedies. Evil Eye. Melancholy. Colds. No. There didn't seem to be anything suitable. Yes, there was. Towards the end of the notebook she found a few lines written down at the time when Granny's hand was already rather shaky. 'If people start getting misty and difficult to see.' Good. Moominmamma read the recipe, which was rather complicated, and started at once to mix the medicine for little Ninny.

The bell came tinkling downstairs, one step at a time, with a small pause between each step. Moomintroll had waited for it all morning. But the silver bell wasn't the exciting thing. That was the paws. Ninny's paws were coming down the steps. They were very small, with anxiously bunched toes. Nothing else of Ninny was visible. It was very odd.

Moomintroll drew back behind the porcelain stove and stared bewitchedly at the paws that passed him on their way to the verandah. Now she served herself some tea. The cup was raised in the air and sank back again. She ate some bread and butter and marmalade. Then the cup and saucer drifted away to the kitchen, were washed and put away in the closet. You see, Ninny was a very orderly little child.

Moomintroll rushed out in the garden and shouted: 'Mamma! She's got paws! You can see her paws!'

I thought as much, Moominmamma was thinking where she sat high in the apple tree. Granny knew a thing or two. Now when the medicine starts to work we'll be on the right way.

'Splendid,' said Moominpappa. 'And better still when she shows her snout one day. It makes me feel sad to talk with people who are invisible. And who never answer me.'

'Hush, dear,' Moominmamma said warningly. Ninny's paws were standing in the grass among the fallen apples.

 'Hello, Ninny,' shouted My. 'You've slept like a

hog. When are you going to show your snout? You must look a fright if you've wanted to be invisible.'

'Shut up,' Moomintroll whispered, 'she'll be hurt.' He went running up to Ninny and said:

'Never mind My. She's hardboiled. You're really safe here among us. Don't even think about that horrid lady. She can't come here and take you away . . .'

In a moment Ninny's paws had faded away and become nearly indistinguishable from the grass.

'Darling, you're an ass,' said Moominmamma. 'You can't go about reminding the kid about those things. Now pick apples and don't talk rubbish.'

They all picked apples.

After a while Ninny's paws became clearer again and climbed one of the trees.

It was a beautiful autumn morning. The shadows made one's snout a little chilly but the sunshine felt nearly like summer. Everything was wet from the night's rain, and all colours were strong and clear. When all the apples were picked or shaken down Moominpappa carried the biggest apple mincer out in the garden, and they started making apple-cheese.

Moomintroll turned the handle, Moominmamma

fed the mincer with apples and Moominpappa carried the filled jars to the verandah. Little My sat in a tree singing the Big Apple Song.

Suddenly there was a crash.

On the garden path appeared a large heap of apple-cheese, all prickly with glass splinters. Beside the heap one could see Ninny's paws, rapidly fading away.

'Oh,' said Moominmamma. 'That was the jar we use to give to the bumble-bees. Now we needn't carry it down to the field. And Granny always said that if you want the earth to grow something for you, then you have to give it a present in the autumn.'

Ninny's paws appeared back again, and above them a pair of spindly legs came to view. Above the legs one could see the faint outline of a brown dress hem.

'I can see her legs!' cried Moomintroll.

'Congrats,' said little My, looking down out of her tree. 'Not bad. But the Groke knows why you must wear snuff-brown.'

Moominmamma nodded to herself and sent a thought to her Granny and the medicine.

Ninny padded along after them all day. They became used to the tinkle and no longer thought Ninny very remarkable.

By evening they had nearly forgotten about her. But when everybody was in bed Moominmamma took out a rose-pink shawl of hers and made it into a little dress. When it was ready she carried it upstairs to the eastern attic room and cautiously laid it out on a chair. Then she made a broad hair ribbon out of the material left over.

Moominmamma was enjoying herself tremendously. It was exactly like sewing doll's clothes again. And the funny thing was that one didn't know if the doll had yellow or black hair.

The following day Ninny had her dress on. She was visible up to her neck, and when she came down to morning tea she bobbed and piped:

'Thank you all ever so much.'

The family felt very embarrassed, and no one found anything to say. Also it was hard to know where to look when one talked to Ninny. Of course one tried to look a bit above the bell where Ninny was supposed to have her eyes. But then very easily one found oneself staring at some of the visible things further down instead, and it gave one an impolite feeling.

Moominpappa cleared his throat. 'We're happy to see,' he started, 'that we see more of Ninny today. The more we see the happier we are . . .'

My gave a laugh and banged the table with her spoon. 'Fine that you've started talking,' she said. 'Hope you have anything to say. Do you know any good games?'

'No,' Ninny piped. 'But I've heard about games.'

Moomintroll was delighted. He decided to teach Ninny all the games he knew.

After coffee all three of them went down to the river to play. Only Ninny turned out to be quite impossible. She bobbed and nodded and very seriously replied, quite, and how funny, and of course, but it was clear to all that she played only from politeness and not to have fun.

'Run, run, can't you!' My cried. 'Or can't you even jump?'

Ninny's thin legs dutifully ran and jumped. Then she stood still again with arms dangling. The empty dress neck over the bell was looking strangely helpless.

'D'you think anybody likes that?' My cried. 'Haven't you any life in you? D'you want a biff on the nose?'

'Rather not,' Ninny piped humbly.

'She can't play,' mumbled Moomintroll.

'She can't get angry,' little My said. 'That's what's wrong with her. Listen, you,' My continued and went close to Ninny with a menacing look. 'You'll never have a face of your own until you've learned to fight. Believe me.'

'Yes, of course,' Ninny replied, cautiously backing away.

There was no further turn for the better.

At last they stopped trying to teach Ninny to play. She didn't like funny stories either. She never laughed at the right places. She never laughed at all, in fact. This had a depressing effect on the person who told the story. And she was left alone to herself.

Days went by, and Ninny was still without a face. They became accustomed to seeing her pink dress marching along behind Moominmamma. As soon as Moominmamma stopped, the silver bell also stopped, and when she continued her way the bell began tinkling again. A bit above the dress a big rose-pink bow was bobbing in thin air.

Moominmamma continued to treat Ninny with Granny's medicine, but nothing further happened. So after some time she stopped the treatment, thinking that many people had managed all right before without a head, and besides perhaps Ninny wasn't very good-looking.

Now everyone could imagine for himself what she looked like, and this can often brighten up a relationship.

One day the family went off through the wood down to the beach. They were going to pull the boat up for winter. Ninny came tinkling behind as usual, but when they came in view of the sea she suddenly stopped. Then she lay down on her stomach in the sand and started to whine.

'What's come over Ninny? Is she frightened?' asked Moominpappa.

'Perhaps she hasn't seen the sea before,' Moominmamma said. She stooped and exchanged a few whispering words with Ninny. Then she straightened up again and said:

'No, it's the first time. Ninny thinks the sea's too big.'

'Of all the silly kids,' little My started, but Moominmamma gave her a severe look and said: 'Don't be a silly kid yourself. Now let's pull the boat ashore.'

They went out on the landing-stage to the bathing hut where Too-ticky lived, and knocked at the door.

'Hello,' Too-ticky said, 'how's the invisible child?'

'There's only her snout left,' Moominpappa replied. 'At the moment she's a bit startled but it'll pass over. Can you lend us a hand with the boat?'

'Certainly,' Too-ticky said.

While the boat was pulled ashore and turned keel upwards Ninny had padded down to the water's edge and was standing immobile on the wet sand. They left her alone.

Moominmamma sat down on the landing-stage and looked down into the water. 'Dear me, how cold it looks,' she said. And then she yawned a bit and added that nothing exciting had happened for weeks.

Moominpappa gave Moomintroll a wink, pulled a horrible face and started to steal up to Moominmamma from behind.

Of course he didn't really think of pushing her in the water as he had done many times when she was young. Perhaps he didn't even want to startle her, but just to amuse the kids a little.

But before he reached her a sharp cry was heard, a pink streak of lightning shot over the landing-stage and Moominpappa let out a scream and dropped his hat into the water. Ninny had sunk her small invisible teeth in Moominpappa's tail, and they were sharp.

'Good work!' cried My. 'I couldn't have done it better myself!'

Ninny was standing on the landing-stage. She had a small, snub-nosed, angry face below a red tangle of hair. She was hissing at Moominpappa like a cat.

'Don't you *dare* push her into the big horrible sea!' she cried.

'I see her, I see her!' shouted Moomintroll. 'She's sweet!'

'Sweet my eye,' said Moominpappa, inspecting his bitten tail. 'She's the silliest, nastiest, badly-brought-uppest child I've ever seen, with or without a head.'

He knelt down on the landing-stage and tried to fish for his hat with a stick. And in some mysterious way he managed to tip himself over, and tumbled in on his head.

He came up at once, standing safely on the bottom, with his snout above water and his ears filled with mud.

'Oh dear!' Ninny was shouting. 'Oh, how great! Oh, how funny!'

The landing-stage shook with her laughter.

'I believe she's never laughed before,' Too-ticky said wonderingly. 'You seem to have changed her, she's even worse than little My. But the main thing is that one can see her, of course.'

'It's all thanks to Granny,' Moominmamma said.

The Last Dragon in the World

ONE Thursday, one of the last of the dog-days, Moomintroll caught a small dragon in the brown pond to the right of Moominpappa's hammock-tree.

Of course he hadn't dreamed of catching a dragon. He had hunted for a few of those small wobbly things that were rowing about in the bottom mud, because he wanted to know how they moved their legs when swimming, and whether they always swam backwards. But when he lifted his glass jar against the light there was something altogether different in it.

'By my everlasting tail,' Moomintroll whispered, overawed. He held the jar between both paws and could only stare.

The dragon was no bigger than a matchbox, and it swam around with graceful strokes of its transparent wings that were as beautiful as the fins of a goldfish.

But no goldfish was as splendidly golden as this miniature dragon. It was sparkling like gold; it was knobbly with gold in the sunlight, the small head was emerald green and its eyes were lemon yellow. The six golden legs had each a green little paw, and the tail turned green towards the tip. It was a truly wonderful dragon.

Moomintroll screwed the lid on the jar (there were breathing-holes) and carefully put it down in the moss. Then he stretched himself out beside the jar and took a closer look.

The dragon swam close to the glass wall and opened its small jaws. They were packed with tiny white teeth.

It's angry, Moomintroll thought. It's angry even if it's so very small. What can I do to make it like me? . . . And what does it eat? What do dragons feed on?

A little worried and anxious he lifted the jar in his arms and started homewards, cautiously, so as not to make the dragon hurt itself against the glass walls. It was so very small and delicate.

'I'll keep you and pet you and love you,' Moomintroll whispered. 'You can sleep on my pillow. When you grow up and start liking me I'll take you for swims in the sea . . .'

Moominpappa was working on his tobacco patch. One could always show him the dragon and ask him about it. Or still, perhaps better not. Not yet. One could keep it a secret for a few days, until it had become used to people. And until one had had the greatest fun of all: showing it to Snufkin.

Moomintroll pressed the jar hard against him and went strolling towards the back door as indifferently as possible. The others were somewhere on the front side by the verandah. At the moment when Moomintroll slunk up the back steps little My jumped into view from behind the water barrel and called:

'What've you got?'

'Nothing,' said Moomintroll.

'A jar,' said My, craning her neck. 'What's in it? Why are you hiding it?'

Moomintroll rushed upstairs and into his room. He put the jar on the table. The water was sloshing about, and the dragon had wound his wings around him and curled up into a ball. Now it slowly straightened out and showed its teeth.

It won't happen again, Moomintroll promised. I'm so sorry, dearest. He screwed off the lid, so as to give the dragon a better view, and then he went to the door and put the latch on. You never knew with My.

When he returned to the dragon it had crawled

out of the water and was sitting on the edge of the jar. Moomintroll cautiously stuck out a paw to fondle it.

At this the dragon opened its jaws again and blew out a small cloud of smoke. A red tongue darted out like a flame and vanished again . . .

'Ow,' said Moomintroll, because he had burned himself. Not much, but distinctly.

He admired the dragon more than ever.

'You're angry, aren't you?' he asked in a low voice. 'You're terribly wild and cruel and wicked, are you, what? Oh you sweet little goody-goody-goo!'

The dragon snorted.

Moomintroll crawled under his bed and pulled out his night box. In it were a couple of small pancakes, now a little dried, half a piece of bread and butter and an apple. He cut small pieces from them all and laid the morsels on the table in a circle around the dragon. It sniffed at them, gave him a contemptuous look and suddenly ran surprisingly nimbly to the window, where it attacked a large August fly.

The fly stopped humming and started to screech. The dragon already had its small green forepaws around its neck and blew a little smoke in its eyes.

And then the small white teeth went snippity-snap, the jaws came open and the August fly disappeared. The dragon swallowed twice, licked its snout, scratched its ear and gave Moomintroll a scoffing, one-eyed glance.

'How clever you are!' cried Moomintroll. 'My little teeny-weeny-poo!'

Just then Moominmamma beat the lunch gong downstairs.

'Now wait for me and be good,' Moomintroll said. 'I'll be back soon.'

He stood for a moment looking longingly at the dragon, that didn't appear to be cuddly in the least. Then he whispered: 'Little dearie,' and ran downstairs and out on the verandah.

Even before her spoon had touched her porridge My started off:

'Certain people seem to be hiding secrets in mysterious glass jars.'

'Shut up,' said Moomintroll.

'One is led to believe,' My continued, 'that certain people are keeping leeches or wood-lice or why not very large centipedes that multiply a hundred times a minute.'

'Mother,' Moomintroll said. 'You know, I've always wished for some small pet that was attached to me, and if I would ever have one, then it should be, or would . . .'

'How much wood would a wood louse chuck,' said My and blew bubbles in her milk glass.

'What?' asked Moominpappa and looked up from his newspaper.

'Moomintroll has found a new animal,' Moominmamma explained. 'Does it bite?'

'It's so small it can't bite very hard,' her son mumbled.

'And when will it grow up?' asked the Mymble. 'When can one have a look at it? Does it talk?'

Moomintroll was silent. Now all was spoiled again. One ought to have the right to have a secret and to spring it as a surprise. But if you live inside a family you have neither. They know about everything from the start, and nothing's any fun after that.

'I'm going down to the river after lunch,' Moomintroll said, slowly and contemptuously. Contemptuously as a dragon. 'Mother, please tell them that they're not to go into my room. I can't answer for the consequences.'

'Good,' said Moominmamma and gave My a look, 'Not a living soul may open his door.'

Moomintroll finished his porridge in dignified silence. Then he went out, through the garden down to the bridge.

Snufkin was sitting before his tent, painting a cork float. Moomintroll looked at him, and straight away he felt happy over his dragon again.

'Whew,' he said. 'Families are a cross sometimes.'

Snufkin grunted in agreement without taking his pipe from his mouth. They sat silent for a while, in male and friendly solidarity.

'By the way,' Moomintroll suddenly said. 'Have you ever come across a dragon on your wanderings?'

'You don't mean salamanders, lizards or crocodiles, apparently,' Snufkin replied after a long silence. 'You mean a dragon. No. Never. They're extinct.'

'But there *might* be one left,' Moomintroll said slowly, 'and someone might even catch it in a glass jar some day.'

Snufkin gave him a sharp look and saw that Moomintroll was about to burst from delight and suspense. So he replied quite curtly:

‘I don’t believe it.’

‘Possibly it would be no bigger than a matchbox even if it could spit fire all right,’ Moomintroll continued with a yawn.

‘Well, that’s pure fantasy, of course,’ said Snufkin, who knew how surprises are prepared.

His friend stared past him and said:

‘A dragon of pure gold with tiny green paws, who’d be devoted to one and follow one everywhere . . .’

And then Moomintroll jumped to his feet and cried:

‘I’ve found it! I’ve found a real dragon of my own!’

While they walked up to the house Snufkin went through the whole scale of disbelief, astonishment and wonder. He was perfect.

They went upstairs, opened the door with great caution and went in.

The jar of water stood on the table as before, but the dragon had disappeared from it. Moomintroll looked under the bed, behind the chest of drawers and all over the floor, calling all the while:

'Little friend . . . my pretty-pretty . . . my teeny-weeny, where are you . . .'

'Moomin,' Snufkin said, 'it's sitting on the window curtain.'

So it was, high on the rod near the ceiling.

'How on earth,' cried Moomintroll in great alarm. 'He mustn't fall down . . . Keep quite still. Wait a bit . . . don't talk . . .'

He pulled the bedclothes from his bed and spread them on the floor below the window. Then he took the hemulen's old butterfly net and reached up towards the dragon.

'Jump!' he whispered. 'Teeny-weeny . . . don't be afraid, it can't hurt you . . .'

'You'll frighten it away,' said Snufkin.

The dragon yawned and hissed. It gave the butterfly net a good bite and started to purr like a small engine. And suddenly it flapped out under the ceiling and began flying around in circles.

'He's flying, he's flying!' Moomintroll shouted. 'My dragon's flying!'

'Of course,' said Snufkin. 'Don't jump about so. Keep still.'

 The dragon was hanging quite still in the air. Its

wings were a blur, like a moth's. And then suddenly it dived down, bit Moomintroll in the ear, so he gave a cry and then it flew straight to Snufkin and settled on his shoulder.

It edged closer against his ear, closed its eyes and started to purr.

'What a funny creature,' Snufkin said in astonishment. 'It's all hot and glowing. What does it do?'

'It's liking you,' said Moomintroll.

In the afternoon the Snork Maiden came home from visiting little My's grandma and of course was told at once that Moomintroll had found a dragon.

It was sitting on the verandah table beside Snufkin's cup of coffee, licking its paws. It had bitten everybody except Snufkin, and every time it became cross at anything it burned a hole somewhere.

'What a sweetie-pie,' said the Snork Maiden. 'What's its name?'

'Nothing special,' Moomintroll mumbled. 'It's just a dragon.'

He let his paw warily crawl across the table until it touched one of the little gilded legs. At once the dragon whirled around, hissed at him and blew a small cloud of smoke.

'How sweet!' the Snork Maiden cried.

The dragon ran over to Snufkin's pipe that was lying at the table, and sniffed at the bowl. Where it had sat was a round brown-edged hole in the table cloth.

'I wonder if it can burn through oilcloth too,' Moominmamma said.

'Naturally,' said little My. 'Just wait until it's grown a bit. It'll burn down the house for us.'

She grabbed a piece of cake, and the dragon rushed at her like a small golden fury and bit her in the paw.

'You d . . . d spider!' cried My, and slapped at the dragon with her napkin.

'If you say things like that you'll never go to heaven,' the Mymble started instantly, but Moomintroll cut her short with a cry:

'It wasn't the dragon's fault! He thought you wanted the fly that was sitting on the cake.'

'You and your dragon!' cried My, whose paw was really hurting badly. 'It isn't yours even, it's Snufkin's, because it likes only him!'

There was a silence.

'Did I hear the small fry squeak,' said Snufkin and rose from the table. 'A few hours more and it'll know where it belongs. Well. Be off. Fly to master!'

But the dragon had settled on Snufkin's shoulder again and clung to it with all six clawed paws, purring all the while like a sewing machine. Snufkin picked it up between thumb and forefinger and put it under the tea-cosy. Then he opened the glass door and went out into the garden.

'Oh, he'll suffocate,' Moomintroll said and lifted the tea-cosy half an inch off the table. The dragon came out like lightning, flew straight to the window and sat there staring after Snufkin, with its paws against the pane. After a little while it began to whine, and its golden colour turned to grey from neck to tail.

'Dragons,' Moominpappa broke the silence, 'disappeared from public consciousness about seventy years ago. I've looked them up in the encyclopaedia. The last to keep alive was the emotional species with strong combustion. They are most stubborn and never change their mind about anything . . .'

'Thanks for the tea,' Moomintroll said and rose from the table. 'I'm going upstairs.'

'Darling, shall we leave your dragon here on the verandah?' Moominmamma asked. 'Or are you taking it along with you?'

Moomintroll didn't reply.

He went to the door and opened it. There was a flash as the dragon swished past him, and the Snork Maiden cried:

'Oh! You won't catch it again! Why did you? I hadn't even looked at it properly yet!'

'Go and look for Snufkin,' Moomintroll said between clenched teeth. 'It will be sitting on his shoulder.'

'My darling,' Moominmamma said sadly. 'My little troll.'

Snufkin had barely got his fishing line baited when the dragon came buzzing and settled on his knee. It nearly tied itself into knots from delight at having found him.

'Well, this is a pretty kettle,' Snufkin said and whisked the creature away. 'Shoo. Be off with you. Go home!'

But of course he knew it was no use. The dragon would never leave him. And for all he knew it could live a hundred years.

Snufkin looked a little sadly at the small shining creature that was doing all it could to attract his attention.

'Yes, you're nice,' he said. 'Yes, it would be fun to have you along. But, don't you see, there's Moomintroll . . .'

The dragon yawned. It flew to his ragged hat brim and curled up to sleep on it. Snufkin sighed and cast his line into the river. His new float bobbed in the current, shining brightly red. He knew that Moomintroll wouldn't like fishing today. The Groke take it all . . .

The hours went by.

The little dragon flew off and caught some flies and returned to sleep on the hat. Snufkin got five roaches and one eel that he let off again because it made such a fuss.

Towards evening a boat came down the river. A youngish hemulen steered.

'Any luck?' he asked.

'So so,' Snufkin replied. 'Going far?'

'Oh, well,' said the hemulen.

'Throw me your painter,' Snufkin said. 'You might have use for a few fish. Swaddle them in damp newspapers and roast them on the embers. It's not too bad.'

'And what do *you* want?' asked the hemulen who wasn't used to presents.

Snufkin laughed and took off his hat with the sleeping dragon.

'Now listen,' he said. 'Take this with you as far as you're going and leave it in some nice place where there are a lot of flies. Fold up the hat to look like a nest, and put it under a bush or something to make this dragon feel undisturbed.'

'A dragon, is it?' the hemulen asked suspiciously. 'Does he bite? How often does one have to feed him?'

Snufkin went into his tent and returned with his old tea-kettle. He shoved a tuft of grass down into it and cautiously let the sleeping dragon down after it. Then he placed the lid firmly on and said:

'You can poke some flies down the nozzle now and then, and pour in a few drops of water sometimes also. Don't mind if the kettle becomes hot. Here you are. After a couple of days you can leave it.'

'That's quite a job for five roaches,' the hemulen

replied sourly and hauled home his painter. The boat started to glide with the current.

'Don't forget the hat,' Snufkin called over the water. 'It's very particular about my hat.'

'No, no, no,' said the hemulen and disappeared round the bend.

'He'll burn his fingers some time,' Snufkin thought. 'Might serve him right.'

Moomintroll came after sundown.

'Hello,' Snufkin said.

'Yippee,' Moomintroll said tonelessly. 'Caught any fish?'

'So so,' Snufkin replied. 'Won't you sit down?'

'Oh, I just happened to pass by,' Moomintroll mumbled.

There was a pause. A new kind of silence, troubled and awkward. Finally Moomintroll asked:

'Does he shine in the dark?'

'Who?'

'Oh, the dragon. I just thought it might be fun to ask if a creep like that shines in the dark.'

'I really don't know,' Snufkin said. 'You'd better go home and take a look.'

‘But I’ve let him out,’ Moomintroll cried. ‘Didn’t he come to you?’

‘Nope,’ Snufkin said, lighting his pipe. ‘Dragons, they do as they like. They’re pretty flighty you know, and if they see a fat fly somewhere they forget everything else. That’s dragons. They’re really nothing much.’

Moomintroll was silent for quite a while. Then he sat down in the grass and said:

‘Perhaps you’re right. Perhaps it was just as well that it went away. Well, yes. I rather think so. Snufkin. That new float of yours. I suppose it looked good in the water. The red one.’

‘Not bad,’ Snufkin said. ‘I’ll make you one. Were you planning to fish tomorrow?’

‘Of course,’ Moomintroll said. ‘Naturally.’

PENGUIN CHILDREN'S 60s

ALI BABA AND THE FORTY THIEVES • *Retold by N. J. Dawood*
THE AMAZING PIPPI LONGSTOCKING • *Astrid Lindgren*
ANNE AT GREEN GABLES • *L. M. Montgomery*
AT THE RIVER-GATES AND
OTHER SUPERNATURAL STORIES • *Philippa Pearce*
CLASSIC GHOST STORIES
CLASSIC NONSENSE VERSE
THE CLOCKWORK MOUSE • *Dick King-Smith*
DEAD MAN'S LANE • *Joan Aiken*
THE DRAGON ON THE ROOF • *Terry Jones*
FOUR GREAT GREEK MYTHS • *Roger Lancelyn Green*
THE GREAT MOUSE PLOT AND
OTHER TALES OF CHILDHOOD • *Roald Dahl*
THE GREAT TIME WARP ADVENTURE • *Jon Scieszka*
THE HOOLIGAN'S SHAMPOO • *Philip Ridley*
KEEP IT IN THE FAMILY • *Anne Fine*
KING ARTHUR'S COURT • *Roger Lancelyn Green*
THE LITTLE MERMAID AND
OTHER FAIRY TALES • *Hans Andersen (Translated by Naomi Lewis)*
LOST DOG AND OTHER STORIES • *Penelope Lively*
THE MIDNIGHT STORY • *Margaret Mahy*
MOOMINTROLLS AND FRIENDS • *Tove Jansson*
MRS PEPPERPOT TURNS DETECTIVE • *Alf Prøysen*
THE NIGHT TRAIN: STORIES IN PROSE AND VERSE • *Allan Ahlberg*
THE PIED PIPER OF HAMELIN AND OTHER CLASSIC STORIES IN VERSE
ROBIN HOOD AND HIS MERRY MEN • *Roger Lancelyn Green*
SHERLOCK HOLMES AND THE SPECKLED BAND • *Sir Arthur Conan Doyle*
SMACKING MY LIPS • *Michael Rosen*
TALES FROM ALICE IN WONDERLAND • *Lewis Carroll*
TALES FROM THE JUNGLE BOOK • *Rudyard Kipling*
THREE QUIRKY TAILS • *Paul Jennings*
TOM SAWYER'S PIRATE ADVENTURE • *Mark Twain*
TOM THUMB AND OTHER FAIRY TALES • *Jacob and Wilhelm Grimm*

Some Puffin books by Tove Jansson

COMET IN MOOMINLAND
THE EXPLOITS OF MOOMINPAPPA
FINN FAMILY MOOMINTROLL
MOOMINLAND MIDWINTER
MOOMINPAPPA AT SEA
MOOMINSUMMER MADNESS
MOOMINVALLEY IN NOVEMBER
TALES FROM MOOMINVALLEY